For Simon and Anna

William Heinemann Ltd
Michelin House
81 Fulham Road
London SW3 6RB

LONDON MELBOURNE AUCKLAND

First published in Great Britain in 1990
Copyright © 1990 Catherine Anholt
0 434 92607 8
Printed in Singapore by
Times Publishing Group

The Snow Fairy
and The Spaceman

Catherine Anholt

HEINEMANN LONDON

There was once a little girl and it was her birthday.
That afternoon she was going to have a very special party.
All her friends were coming in fancy dress.
Her mother had made her a beautiful fairy costume with
wings, a crown and a silver wand.

Just as she was dressing for the party it began to snow.
"I must be a snow fairy," she told her father as he pinned on
her silver wings.
Then she ran downstairs to show her dress to her mother.

"Look at me, I'm a snow fairy!" she called.
"Don't you look lovely," said her mother, "but those shoes are rather big for you."
"They're *not*. I like them!" said the snow fairy.

At three o'clock there was a knock at the door and in came
a lion, a robot, a king and an alligator . . .

. . . a clown, a butterfly, a wizard, a sunflower and a very small
and rather shy spaceman. Each of them was carrying a present.

The snow fairy quickly opened all the parcels. She unwrapped a paintbox, a doll, a book and a teddy.
When the spaceman gave her his present she was very rude. It was another paintbox!
"I've already got one of those," she said, not even thanking him. And she ran off into the sitting room.

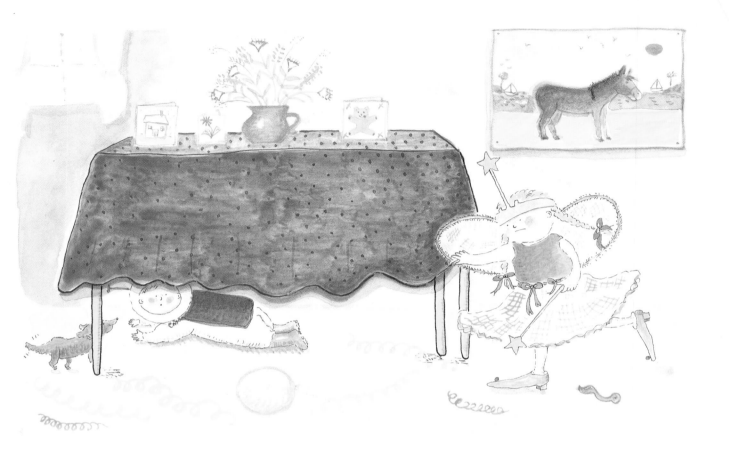

The spaceman wasn't really sure he liked parties, and he didn't want to join in when the noisy children ran round playing Follow the Leader.

When it was his turn to be blindfolded to play 'Pin the Tail on the Donkey,' he hid under the table.

"What's the matter with you? Come on," said the snow fairy.

Suddenly a balloon popped and the spaceman burst into tears.
The other children turned and stared at him.
"What's the matter *now*," said the snow fairy.

And she ran off and popped another balloon with her wand.
The spaceman felt very miserable.
He wished his mother would come and take him home.
So when no one was looking he crept into the garden.

"Let's play Hide and Seek," shouted the lion.
"All right," said the snow fairy's mother.
"But stay in the house, it's too cold to go outside."
"It's my birthday. Let me hide first," said the snow fairy.
The children covered their eyes and began to count.
"1 2 3 4 5 6 7 8 9 10 11 12 13 14 15 16 17 18 19 20 . . . coming!"
they called.

The snow fairy was nowhere to be seen. The lion looked in the living room. The robot looked in the rubbish bin. The king looked in the kitchen. The alligator looked in the attic.

The clown looked in the cupboard. The butterfly looked in the bath. The sunflower looked behind the sofa. The wizard looked in the wardrobe. But they couldn't find her anywhere . . . because she was in the garden!

"No one will find me here," she laughed as she ran across the
snow to the treehouse.
She hadn't seen the little spaceman sitting on a tree stump
looking rather lonely.

She leapt up the ladder, but it wasn't easy to climb because it was covered in ice and her shoes were far too big. She was just about to scramble into the treehouse, WHEN . . .

. . . a dreadful thing happened. The ladder slipped and the
snow fairy began to fall. Her shoes fell off and her wings
caught on a branch and left her dangling in mid-air. The
spaceman had been watching it all.
"Are you trying to fly?" he asked politely.
"No I'm not. I'm stuck. Get me down," she shouted.

The spaceman picked up the ladder and carefully climbed up
to untangle her. When they were both safely on the ground,
he handed back her slippery shoes and broken wand.
Then the snow fairy did something rather surprising.
She leaned over and gave him a big kiss, right on the side of
his space helmet.

"Come on," she said, grabbing his hand. "I'm hungry. Let's go and have tea."

The children, tired of looking, were just sitting down to tea.
"Oh, good. There you are," said the sunflower. "You must
have been hiding in a very clever place. Who found you?"
The snow fairy and the spaceman just smiled at each other and
sat down.
"This party is really great," said the spaceman.
The snow fairy grinned. "Bet you're glad you came," she said.
And he was.